Home for Meow

Kitten Around

Reese Eschmann

Scholastic Inc.

Copyright © 2022 by Charisse Eschmann

All rights reserved. Published by Scholastic Inc., *Publishers since 1920.* SCHOLASTIC and associated logos are trademarks and/or registered trademarks of Scholastic Inc.

The publisher does not have any control over and does not assume any responsibility for author or third-party websites or their content.

No part of this publication may be reproduced, stored in a retrieval system, or transmitted in any form or by any means, electronic, mechanical, photocopying, recording, or otherwise, without written permission of the publisher. For information regarding permission, write to Scholastic Inc., Attention: Permissions Department, 557 Broadway, New York, NY 10012.

This book is a work of fiction. Names, characters, places, and incidents are either the product of the author's imagination or are used fictitiously, and any resemblance to actual persons, living or dead, business establishments, events, or locales is entirely coincidental.

Library of Congress Cataloging-in-Publication Data available

ISBN 978-1-338-78400-8

10 9 8 7 6 5 4 3 2 1   22 23 24 25 26

Printed in the U.S.A.   40

First edition, September 2022

Book design by Stephanie Yang

Table of Contents

1

Cat Pies

I blow a huge puff of air through the bubble wand in my hand. It makes big, soapy bubbles that float around the café. One of them lands on a customer's nose. *Oops.* Another bubble lands on the customer's shoe. My family's cat, Pepper, pounces on the shoe and pops the bubble with

her paw. The customer looks startled at first,
then smiles when he sees her gray-and-white
tail swishing back and forth.

"Pepper, be careful!" I laugh. "You'll get bubbles
all over our customers."

Bubbles, a big brown-and-black-striped cat,
leaps over to me when she hears her name. She

sits in front of the bubble wand, waiting for me to blow into it again.

"I know exactly what you're thinking, Bubbles," I say. "You're thinking, *Kira Parker, how do you come up with so many great ideas?* Well, this one was easy! Your name is Bubbles, so I knew you'd love bubbles. It's just simple math."

Bubbles meows at me. I don't think either of us knows much about math. I scratch behind her ears, and she purrs. Bubbles is living at my family's cat café, The Purrfect Cup, until she goes to her fur-ever home. Lots of cats from the animal shelter come to live with us until they can be adopted, but Bubbles is one of the most special cats ever because she gave birth to six kittens! I found adoptive homes for all the kittens, and now Bubbles is going to become a part of our family forever—because my granny is adopting her this weekend!

I look at the clock in the café. It's shaped like a cat. All the numbers are in a circle around the cat's belly, and its tail swings back and forth to announce a new hour. The cat says it's almost five o'clock. That means Granny should be arriving soon! She said she'd be here right after the café closes at five. I have so many *great ideas* for Granny's visit. I'm going to teach her all about how to care for a cat. And I can show her how to use the bubble wand.

I want to tell Mama all about my ideas—I don't think I can wait until Granny gets here to share them! Mama is standing behind the register at the back of the café. In front of her is a long, long line of customers. The line weaves around the tables, cozy seats, and cat beds that fill the café. The customers smile and take pictures of the cats in the café while they wait. Mama told me that the line is so long because business at the café is booming!

Mama runs our café's business, and she's really good at it. She wanted to increase The Purrfect Cup's *social media presence*, which means she started posting pictures of Dad's baked goods online. Dad is the best baker in the whole world!

A lot of people liked Mama's photo of his mini cat-shaped blueberry pies. Pepper and I were excited because we thought the pies were for the cats. Turns out they're for humans only. But now lots of customers are traveling from other towns and waiting in long lines to get a taste!

"Hey, Mama," I say, running up to the register. "Can I tell you about my ideas for Granny's visit? I'm going to read eight books about cats to her, show her how to clean out a litter box using only one hand, and then—"

"Sorry, Kira, can this wait?" Mama asks. She presses her apron to her forehead. "We're swamped right now. I need to help this customer."

The café doesn't look like a swamp. I don't see any alligators. But it does look busier than ever. I thought that was a good thing, but Mama looks so tired.

"I can help take customers' orders!" I say. That should cheer Mama up. "I had this idea about building a robot that can take ten orders at once—"

"How about you go upstairs and help Ryan make Granny's bed? That would help me so much, Kira."

"Okay," I say. I feel a little disappointed. I wanted to help Mama in the *café*, not upstairs in our apartment! Plus, making beds is so hard. My little brother, Ryan, and I always get tangled up in the stretchy sheets, and Pepper loves to hide under the covers while I'm trying to smooth them out. I grab Pepper and Bubbles to head upstairs, but not before turning back to Mama.

"Can I tell you and Dad about my *great ideas* later?" I ask. Mama and Dad haven't had much time for my ideas lately.

"Sure," Mama says, but she doesn't sound so sure. "But your dad is probably going to be up all night again making pies."

The café kitchen is right behind the register at the back of the café. The door to the kitchen is open, and I can see Dad inside. He's hunched over a giant mixer that's spraying flour all over the place! He's been baking nonstop for days. Maybe he wants to trade places with me. I can make pies, and he can make the bed. But before I can ask him, the door to the café swings open, and the smell of vanilla perfume reaches my nostrils. Granny is here early!

Dad always says that Granny likes to make an entrance. That doesn't mean that she builds doors. It means that she makes sure everyone, even the doors, is paying attention to her when she shows up.

She twirls into the café in a big leopard-print coat. "Kira!" she says, loud enough for all the customers to hear. "Look at my grandbaby, all grown up! I bet you're running this place by now, aren't you?"

I smile. I know I'm not running the café.

But maybe I could.

2

Vacation Pants

"Granny!" I shout. I run up to her and give her a big hug. She pulls me into the softness of her coat, and her vanilla perfume fills my nose with sweetness. I remember that I'm holding Pepper and Bubbles.

"Pepper, you remember Granny, right?" I

ask. "We visited her a few months ago."

I don't think Pepper likes the long road trips we take to Granny's house every few months. And she looks a little suspicious of Granny's leopard-print coat. But I know it's not made from *real* leopards. Granny loves cats, even the big ones! Bubbles doesn't seem scared at all, though. She jumps right into Granny's arms and buries her face in the soft fabric of the coat.

"This is Bubbles!" I say. "She's so excited to live with you, Granny."

"That's my girl," Granny says to Bubbles. "We're going to have a good time together, aren't we? Two mamas living the retired life."

I smile. Granny looks at the long line of customers.

"What are all these people doing here?" she asks. "Aren't you about to close?"

"Yeah, but Mama and Dad say that anyone who's in here by five should get to order, even if that means they have to work late."

"Hmm." Granny purses her lips and gives the customers a disapproving look. I don't blame her. I wish Mama and Dad didn't have to work late too.

I sit on the floor in the corner of the café and Granny drags over a chair to join me as we wait for Mama and Dad to finish serving cat pies to all the customers. Ryan comes to sit by us too.

"Did you make Granny's bed?" I whisper in his ear. "Sorry, I was supposed to help you."

Ryan shakes his head. "I gave up," he whispers back. "The sheets got too tangled. So I just took a nap on top of them. I feel great!"

Granny overhears us. "Good for you, Ryan," she says. "You're a growing boy, you need your rest. And besides, I prefer to make my own bed."

Ryan smiles in relief and asks to borrow the bubble wand.

It takes a whole thirty minutes for Mama and Dad to finish serving all the customers! At least I get plenty of time to teach Granny how to blow bubbles for the cats to chase. She blows a bubble almost as big as Ryan's head, which is huge.

Both Pepper and Bubbles run after the bubble. They jump into the air at the same time, then POP! Their noses push against the bubble, popping it as the two of them fall to the ground in a tangle of soapy cat whiskers and flailing paws. Granny throws her head back and laughs so hard her wig almost flies off!

When the last customer leaves, Mama lets out a huge sigh and rests her head on the register. Dad comes out from the kitchen covered in flour.

Granny stands up and puts her hands on her hips. "Are you telling me I had to wait thirty minutes to give my son a hug? And now when I finally see him, he's a mess! I'm not getting flour all over my new coat."

Dad chuckles. "Hey, Mom," he says. "Good to see you too. I'll go change my clothes, and then I can give you that hug."

"Now, hold on just a second," Granny says. "Look at the two of you! When's the last time you took a break? Or even a day off?"

Mama and Dad look at each other. "It has been awhile . . ." Mama says. "The café has just been so busy."

"Well, that's decided, then," Granny says, taking off her coat. "Me and the kids are going to clean up this mess. And while we do that, the two of you can pack."

"Pack?" Dad asks. "Mom, what are you talking about?"

"I'm already here for the weekend," Granny says. "I can run the café and watch the kids. You two are going on a little vacation. You look like you need it."

Dad raises his eyebrows at Mama, but she shakes her head.

"Thanks for offering," Mama says. "But we can't leave the café. I already have a headache thinking about all the things I need to do this weekend—"

"That's exactly why you need to get out of town," Granny says. "Give your brain a break."

"But I'm the only one who knows how to run the register and keep the books, and—"

Granny purses her lips. "I raised your father

and his three troublemaking sisters on my own," she says. "You think I can't handle using a register and counting some money?"

"Are you sure?" Mama sighs. "A vacation does sound nice ... but running the café is a lot of work!"

"Pfft," Granny says, pushing up her sleeves. "What do you young people know about work?"

She winks at me. "What do you think, Kira? Is this a good idea?"

"I think it's *great!*"

♥ 🐾 ♥

Two hours later, the café is spotless and Mama and Dad are about to leave. They're going to stay at a bed-and-breakfast, which is a place where they give you a bed and a breakfast. I told Mama that we already have both of those things here, but she said that the place they're going is nicer than a regular house. Dad says it's even on a farm where they make fresh cheese and have lots of animals! I started to get a little jealous, but then Ryan reminded me that Pepper hates goats. I wouldn't want to go anywhere without Pepper. Not even for cheese.

Dad looks sad to be leaving Pepper too. He holds her in his arms the way people hold a baby. She purrs as he rocks her back and forth.

Pepper is like Dad's third child—and I think she might be his favorite.

"I'm going to miss you so much, Kira and

Ryan," Dad says as he nuzzles his nose against Pepper's nose.

"Uh, Dad, it kinda seems like you're talking to Pepper, not us," I say.

Ryan crosses his arms. "How come you never pick me up like that anymore?"

Dad laughs. "Because that would give me a

backache for a week, and Pepper is such a purrfect wittle baby."

"Dad, you're only going to be gone for the weekend," I say, taking Pepper from his arms. I'm the biggest cat person there ever was. If being a huge cat person meant you were actually huge, I'd be the size of a building! But this is too much, even for me. "You'll be back on Sunday. I bet Pepper won't even notice you're gone! She's my best friend, after all."

Dad leans down to give me, Pepper, and Ryan a kiss on the head. "I'm going to miss all three of you," he says.

"Uh, aren't you forgetting a few family members?" I ask.

Dad looks around at all the cats snoozing on shelves and in baskets. "I mean, I'll miss all *twenty* of you."

Mama walks downstairs into the café from our family's apartment upstairs. She's carrying her suitcase and wearing purple sweatpants with yellow stripes. Dad smiles when he sees her.

"I see you've got your vacation pants on," he says. "We're ready to go!"

Granny comes out from the café kitchen and shakes her head at Mama. "I'll never under-stand those pants," she says. "Ugliest things I've ever seen."

"Mom!" Dad says to Granny. "We don't

use language like that in this house."

Granny shrugs and winks at me. "House rules don't apply to grandmas."

I hold Pepper in front of my face so Dad can't see me laughing. I'll miss Mama and Dad while they're away for the weekend, but I don't mind staying behind. With Mama and Dad gone, I'll be pretty much in charge of The Purrfect Cup. I've had so many *great ideas* about how to make the café even better, but Mama and Dad have been so busy I haven't been able to talk about them. Now I'll finally be able to make my ideas happen *fur real!*

"While we're gone, Granny will be in charge, of course," Mama says. "Kira and Ryan, she's going to need lots of help with the café. But you need to make sure to let her be the leader, okay?"

I frown. Granny is our *granny*, so of course she's in charge. I know that. But I don't know why Mama doesn't want me to be the leader. After all, I know a lot about running the café and I *definitely* know more about cats. I've lived here my whole life!

Dad nods, agreeing with Mama. "Remember to listen to your grandma and help her out as much as you can. And listen to each other too; that's just as important. Otherwise your mama and I will never leave you alone again. Not even when you turn eighteen."

"I wanted to be in charge! I could be the man of the house," Ryan grumbles.

"That's not something we do around here," Dad says. "Your mama and I are equal partners. Just like you and Kira."

Ryan crumples up his face and scowls. Dad crouches down and puts his hand on Ryan's shoulder. "Being equal partners with your sister doesn't make you less of a man, Ryan. It makes you more of one. I know you two bicker sometimes, but I love that you respect each other."

Ryan narrows his eyes at me, like he's trying to figure out if I really respect him. I give him a thumbs-up. Ryan sticks his tongue out at me, then sighs.

"All right," he says. "Equal partners."

I smile. "I hope you're ready, partner," I say. "I have so many great ideas for the café!"

He groans. "Oh no, this weekend is going to be a disaster, isn't it?"

"Don't you mean a dis-*cat*-ster?" I say, nudging Ryan on the shoulder.

He tugs on Mama's striped sweatpants. "Take me with you, please," he begs.

"Relax, Ryan," I say. "I bet you don't even know what a real disaster looks like. You weren't alive during the Great Café Flood of 2003. And neither was I! This weekend is going to be *great*."

"I'm sure it will be great, Kira," Mama says. "Maybe hold off on the great ideas, though. You can tell Dad and me about them when we get home. But it'll be easier for everyone if you stick to what you know this weekend and listen to Granny."

I frown. No *great ideas*? I don't understand why Mama doesn't want me to try out any new ideas. She usually loves them! Maybe she doesn't trust me. But I'm almost nine—I know how to run a café! When I get to be Mama's age, I want to be just like her, with a cat café and a booming business. I wish there was a way to prove to her that I can do it!

"Remember, Mr. Anderson is right next door," Mama continues. "He's available if you need anything. The café opens at eight o'clock tomorrow. And don't forget to feed the cats before the customers arrive, or they'll be all over the baked goods!"

"Speaking of baked goods, what'd you think when you looked at the kitchen, Mom?" Dad asks Granny. "I was in there all day—and all last night—baking cat pies for the weekend crowds."

Last night, I offered to help Dad in the kitchen. I *love* baking, even though my cakes don't always come out the way the recipe is supposed to. Yesterday, when I was making pie dough, I accidentally added melted butter instead of cold butter. When I put my pies into the oven, they turned into a burnt, gloopy mess!

After that, Dad said maybe I should take a little break from baking.

Dad looks at Granny. "Think there's enough food back there to get you through the weekend?"

"I thought your banana bread looked a little dry," Granny says. "And you didn't add enough frosting to the carrot cake. And I'm not so sure about those mini pies. There's not enough blueberry filling in them! What's wrong with the recipe I gave you? That one was perfect."

Dad sighs. "That's not what I was asking, Mom," he says, putting his arm around Granny. "But thanks for keeping me in check."

Granny chuckles. Just then, the door to the

café opens. My best human friend, Alex, walks in. Her mom, Mrs. Patel, waves from the doorway.

"Hey, Alex," I say. "Did you hear my parents are going out of town for the weekend?"

"Yeah! Your mom called my mom to talk about it." She grins, then kneels down to scratch some of the cats' ears. "You're basically going to be in charge of the café! I was doing some research before we came over. Did you know there's a fourteen-year-old who owns his own restaurant in Georgia? You could be like him!"

"That's what I was thinking!" I say, lowering my voice. "But Mama thinks I shouldn't try out any new ideas this weekend."

Mama walks up behind me to say hello to Mrs. Patel. "Want me to make you something to drink?"

Mrs. Patel waves at Mama impatiently. "No, no, I don't need anything! I've got my own tea right here. I just came to make sure that you were *actually* on your way out. You two deserve this vacation! You should get going."

Mama sighs, looking around the café. "Thank you," she says. "We *are* leaving. The bed-and-breakfast is two hours away, and we don't want to get there too late. I was just telling them everything they need to know. But I swear I'm forgetting something . . ."

"You never forget anything," Mrs. Patel assures

her. "You're the most organized woman in the world. Come on, now, my allergies are acting up! I don't want to stand in this doorway forever."

"Okay, okay," Mama says. "We're coming."

"And you have to promise me you're going to turn your phones off for a little bit this weekend. It won't be a real vacation if you're always texting and calling to check in. I'll be around if anything happens at the café. Remember, I'm on the town council now," Mrs. Patel says. "Nothing goes wrong under my nose."

Mrs. Patel sneezes.

Mama and Dad look at each other. "Maybe we'll turn our phones off tomorrow," Dad says hesitantly. "For a little while."

"Good!" Mrs. Patel says. "You two go off and have a nice weekend. I've got a busy one! The town council put me in charge of planning an event for the community. So me and Alex will be doing a lot of research."

"That sounds fun," I say to Alex. "You and your mom should come do your research at the café!"

Alex nods excitedly. "I'll tell her to take extra allergy medicine so we can come by."

Mama and Dad do one more walk-through of the café, then give us another hug before leaving. The bell rings as the door to the café opens and shuts. Granny locks it behind them. Mama and Dad and the Patels are gone.

"Whew," Granny says. "Those two make me

feel like I need a vacation. I thought they'd never leave!"

She picks up Bubbles, who closes her eyes and yawns so wide that I can see all the pointy teeth in her mouth. It makes her look like a roaring lion, but I know she's not about to go hunting. She's just sleepy.

"Me and Bubbles are ready to relax," Granny says. "Want to watch a movie?"

"Can we have popcorn?" I ask.

"And candy?" Ryan adds.

"Of course," Granny says. "I'm here on this earth for one reason and one reason only: to spoil my grandbabies. You can have anything you want."

I raise an eyebrow. "Anything?"

Granny winks at me again. "What's that you were saying about *great ideas* earlier? This café could use a little pick-me-up."

My mouth drops open in excitement. Granny still wants me to use my ideas! Maybe this is how I'll show Mama that I know how to run a café just like she does. I'll *jam-pack* this weekend with a whole bunch of ideas. Dad told me about jam-packing things. It means that you stuff a lot of things into one space, like when you boil a big pot of strawberries and sugar together until they become sweet, simmering jam, and then you pack the jam into a jar. Or like when you stuff so much strawberry jam on your peanut butter and jelly sandwich that it soaks through and the bread turns pink. That's what I'm going to do. I'm going to stuff so many of my ideas into this weekend that it becomes Kira colored. When Mama comes home, she'll see how awesome all my ideas are! Then she'll know that I can help her with more than making the bed.

I can't wait!

3

Kira in Charge

Bright and early on Saturday morning, I plug in my first great idea and turn it all the way up. It's a big stereo that Dad usually keeps in the basement. Ryan and I dragged it upstairs and wiped all the dust off. Now it's working perfectly! Mama usually plays soft piano music in the café from a small speaker connected to her phone. She calls it "neutral" music because it doesn't bother anyone. It's like the color gray. But the color gray is BORING! I'd rather have music that makes me want to dance and sing.

"Is this one of my old records?" Granny asks as she and Ryan come down into the café. "I gave them to your father, but I thought he never played them. They don't make music like this anymore."

Granny moves along with the rhythm. All the cats in the café turn to stare at the stereo. They tilt their heads back and forth, and some of them even stand up on their back two legs to get a better look! When Mama sees how much the cats love this music, she'll be so impressed. My great ideas are already working!

"Look, the cats are dancing too!" I say.

"Either that or they're getting ready to attack you," Ryan says. "Can you turn that down?"

"You're only annoyed because you don't know how to dance," I say.

"I do know how to dance, I just only like to do it when I'm alone and all the lights are off."

Granny grabs Ryan's hands and twirls him around. "C'mon, baby, don't be shy!" she says. Then she stops and puts a hand on her lower back. "Ooh, I need to slow down. Who's that?"

Granny looks out the window. Mr. Anderson

and his husband, Ben, are waving at us from outside the café. Mr. Anderson owns the craft store next door, and he's one of our cats' favorite customers. I unlock the door for him and Ben.

"Good morning!" I say. "We're going to open soon. Do you two want to be the first customers at The Purrfect Cup 2.0?"

"The Purrfect Cup 2.0?" Ben says. "What's that?"

"It's The Purrfect Cup, plus a little extra Kira-and-Ryan magic!" I say.

"Well, that sounds exciting," Mr. Anderson says, looking over my head into the café. "I can't wait to see what the magic is. But we were actually just coming over to make sure everything was okay. We heard a lot of noise, and it's pretty early in the morning."

"That's our new café music!" I say. "Don't you love it? It's not neutral at all, right?"

Mr. Anderson shakes his head. "It's really not."

Behind Mr. Anderson, I spot a woman and a boy my age walking by on the sidewalk. They stop and turn to look at us standing in the doorway. "Ooh, I love this song," the woman says, clapping in time with the music. "What's the name of this place?"

I smile wide and stand up on my tiptoes. I'm already getting new customers!

"This is The Purrfect Cup," I say. "The best and only cat café in town. You can come dance and eat cat pies and play with the cutest cats in the world!"

"How can I say no to that?" The woman laughs.

The boy runs up to the window and presses his nose against it. "Holy moly, there are a lot of cats in there! Can we go inside, Nanay?"

"We have to run some errands, but we'll come back in the afternoon with the whole family," the woman says. "They'll love this place!"

I wave goodbye as they walk down the street.

"So, Kira, about the noise..." Mr. Anderson says, but before he can finish his sentence, the music shuts off.

"Come inside," Granny calls from the back of the café. She sets two steaming cups of coffee on the counter. "You two look tired. We're sorry if our music woke you up. But you know my Kira loves a little joy in the morning."

Mr. Anderson smiles. "No problem," he says, taking a big gulp of coffee.

Oops. I didn't realize the music was that loud. "Sorry," I say. "I didn't mean to wake you up. Will you be sleeping this afternoon when that family comes by?"

Mr. Anderson laughs. "No, I think we'll be awake then. And we'd love to hear some of your joyful music."

"Can we get you anything else?" Ryan asks. His voice sounds very proper. I notice for the first time that he's wearing a suit! "We have many tasty treats here at The Purrfect Cup. Blueberry cat pies, snickerdoodles, cups of whipped cream..."

"I wouldn't say no to a cat pie," Ben says.

"They're a little dry," Grandma warns. "There's not enough filling."

"I'll get it!" I say, running to the kitchen. I wash my hands, then wrap up two freshly warmed mini cat-shaped pies for Ben and Mr. Anderson. I take a big bite out of a third pie. It doesn't taste dry to me! Dad is the best baker in the whole world. The crust is flaky and buttery, and the blueberry filling is sweet and a little bit lemony. It's perfect.

I give the cat pies to Ben and Mr. Anderson.

First customers, served! Now we have to get ready for the café to open. I feel as excited as I did that time Mama let me put a lemonade stand in the middle of the café. I sold a lot of lemonade that day. I spilled a lot of it too, but the cats loved the sticky-sweet floors.

"Hey, partner, want to hear my other *great*

ideas?" I ask Ryan. We're setting rows of cat pies in the bakery case next to the counter. Granny is counting the money in the register.

"Sure," he says. "But I can't believe you didn't dress like a businessperson. You look like normal Kira!"

I look down at my cat-print sweatshirt and my smudged shoes. "This is my lucky outfit!" I protest. "I need it for my *great ideas.* Besides, Mama and Dad don't wear suits every day. Wearing fancy clothes doesn't mean you have a fancy brain. Dad's clothes are always covered in flour, but he's still the best baker in the world."

Ryan raises an eyebrow at me. "Didn't Mama say to hold off on the ideas?"

"Well, yes..." I say. "But Granny said the café could use some fresh ideas. And Mama said Granny is in charge, so I think we should listen to her. When Mama gets back and she sees how awesome my ideas are, she won't be upset. She'll be proud!"

Ryan shrugs. "In that case, I have a few *great ideas* too. I think we should close the shop a few times a day so the cats can take naps and play. There have been way too many people in here. Sometimes the cats want time to themselves! Cats need cat naps. Also, I think we should write biographies about the cats. We could leave the biographies around the café so the customers could get to know them better. Then they might adopt them!"

"I think you mean you want some time to have the cats all to yourself," I say. "We won't make any money if the café is closed! But I like the idea of cat biographies. I was also thinking that we should put cupcakes out now, instead of waiting until after lunch. People love pie and cake for breakfast! And we should let the customers decorate the cupcakes themselves! We could also sell T-shirts and cute cat photos."

Ryan scratches his chin. "Not bad, not bad," he says. "I could get on board with that."

There's not much time left before the café opens. Ryan and I spend the rest of it making cupcake decoration cups to sell. We fill the cups with sprinkles, edible glitter, and small candies. Then Granny lets us have a cupcake for breakfast.

"I set up the register and got all the coffee ready," Granny says proudly. "And Bubbles and I both did our business. She went in the litter box right next to the toilet. Is there anything else we need to do before we open? I'm exhausted. I don't know how your parents do this every day."

"I think we're ready to open!" I say.

We turn on all the lights, and Ryan turns around the sign on the front door. It has pictures of paw prints and coffee mugs on it, and it says:

Welcome to The Purrfect Cup!

Come On In, We're Open!

A few minutes later, a man walks through the door carrying a big, boxy bag. I recognize his red beard right away. His name is Peter, and he works at the King County Animal Shelter. That's where Mama and Dad get all the cats who live at The Purrfect Cup. Peter takes care of them until they come home with us.

"Good morning, Peter!" I say. "Can I interest you in a cat pie or a breakfast cupcake?"

"Are you going to fill that whole bag with cat pies?" Ryan asks. "You should know they're not actually for cats, so you can't share them with the animals at the shelter. You'd have to eat them all yourself."

Peter laughs. "Actually, I have a delivery for you!"

He zips the bag open. A huge, fuzzy white cat jumps out—and lands right on Granny's head!

4

Big Personalities

"You guys really didn't know you were getting a new cat today?" Peter says. He was surprised when we told him that Mama and Dad are out of town.

"We didn't know a thing," Granny says. "But my daughter-in-law did say she was forgetting

to tell us something. I thought she was forgetting to tell me how much I'm getting paid for
working this weekend!"

"It's okay," I say. "We love getting new cats!"

I reach out to pet the big white cat, but she
thinks I'm trying to play with her and rolls
over onto her back. She paws at my hand and
wriggles around on the floor. Then she bumps
into a basket. The cat inside meows loudly and
runs away.

"Well, I should mention that she has a, um ...
big personality," Peter says.

Uh-oh. That's what my kindergarten teacher
said about me when I got caught sneaking
kittens into school in my backpack. She said it

again when I gave cat food to all my friends on Halloween. I just wanted them to be ready in case they ever saw a hungry kitten!

"I'm sure she'll fit in great," I say. "We love big personalities here!"

"That's true," Granny says. "Mine is huge."

"She really likes attention," Peter warns. "And she's a little clumsy."

"Don't worry," Ryan says. "Kira is also clumsy."

I make a face at him before turning back to Peter with a confident smile. "Granny is right," I say. "This is The Purrfect Cup 2.0, and we LOVE big personalities! We've got everything under control. Does she have a name?"

"We've been calling her Dozer. But not because

she sleeps a lot. She's more like, you know...a bulldozer."

With that, Peter leaves. Ryan drags a string around the café, and Dozer chases him in a circle. The other cats look suspicious. They all climb onto shelves and cat trees to avoid the newest member of our cat family. Usually, Mama takes at least a few days to slowly introduce new cats in the café. But we don't have enough people to watch the café *and* watch Dozer upstairs!

Soon Ryan is out of breath from running around. "This cat has a LOT of energy," he yells, laughing.

Granny is fixing her makeup in front of the

mirror behind the register. Bubbles sits next to her, licking her paw. I'm glad Granny and Bubbles are getting along. I didn't even need to read Granny eight cat books! She and Bubbles were instant BFFs.

"Man oh man, I look GOOD, don't I?" Granny asks. "None of the other grandmas look as good as me, that's for sure. Your customers aren't going to know what hit 'em!"

"You look beautiful, Granny," I say. "But I think you forgot your dentures."

Granny smiles wide. "I sure did! Bring me my teeth, baby. They're upstairs on the bathroom counter."

I run upstairs to grab them. When I come back

downstairs, there are four customers in the café! I take their orders.

"Two of our famous cat pies, one peach scone, and one breakfast cupcake with a sprinkles cup," I say. I smile at the last customer. "Good choice!"

I knew the customers would love DIY breakfast cupcakes! I'm sure Mama is going to want to keep using this idea. Maybe she'll even put me in charge of it!

Ryan helps the customers to their seats while I get the food ready. Granny pours their coffee. Pepper sits on my shoulder and sniffs at the food as I bring it to the tables.

"Pepper," I whisper. "Be careful. We don't want

these customers to think there's cat hair in their food."

But when I set the cupcake down on the table in front of the last customer, Pepper jumps off my shoulder. She sits on the table. She's too close to the customer and too close to the cupcake! But she doesn't listen when I ask her to move. She's so focused on the cupcake that she sits very, very still. She almost looks like a statue.

"Is this normal?" the customer asks.

"Uh, there is no normal at The Purrfect Cup," I say. "That's one of its charms! Cats love to surprise you—whoa."

One by one, the cats who were sitting high up on shelves jump down. They get closer and closer to the four customers, their eyes on the food. They move carefully and slowly, like lions hunting prey in the wild.

"What's going on?" Ryan whispers, his eyes wide.

Granny's looking at her dentures in the mirror. "Hey, Kira," she says casually. "What was that thing your mama said we needed to do before we opened the café?"

"Feed the cats," I say. I completely forgot. My stomach flips over. Maybe a cupcake for breakfast wasn't such a good idea.

♥ 🐾 ♥

Before I can stop her, Dozer jumps up onto the table next to Pepper and licks the customer's cupcake. She doesn't even seem guilty after-ward! She looks up at me like she thinks I'm going to be proud of her.

"Dozer! No!" I say sternly, but she takes another lick. Pepper hisses, but I think it's because she wants frosting too, not because she's mad at Dozer.

"Ryan, go get the cat food!" I say.

"But how are we going to feed the cats?" he asks. "There are already customers here."

"We'll just feed them with the customers here," I say. "I mean, it *is* a cat café. There should be cat food. Hey, maybe we should sell it! Wouldn't that be a *great idea*?"

Ryan doesn't look so sure, but he runs to get

the cat food anyway. I apologize to the customer and bring him another cupcake. But first I shoo Pepper and Dozer. Pepper hops off the table, and Dozer thinks she's trying to play. She jumps right on top of her! Pepper sprints away and hides behind the counter with Granny and Bubbles.

Granny looks at her watch. "You know, I think it's late enough to turn the music back on."

She turns up the dial on Dad's stereo. As soon as the music comes on, Dozer stops in her tracks. She leaves the other cats alone and runs over to the stereo. Dozer hops on top and sways with the music. Her body vibrates with the booming bass. Then she lies down and starts blinking slowly.

"Granny! She's falling asleep!" I exclaim. "She loves music. I think it makes her feel calm."

I understand that. When I'm feeling nervous or too excited, I love to draw and make art. Ryan likes to make a fort out of all the pillows in the apartment—including *mine*—and take long naps inside. And Alex told me that when she's nervous, she likes to read her favorite books over and over again. I guess everyone—even cats— has something they do that helps them calm down. Dozer's thing is music!

When Ryan comes back, we empty cans of cat food onto plates. I set the plates on the café tables and leave a few cans in the bakery case so I can sell them to customers. After all, they're here to see the cats! Shouldn't they want to feed them? If they have a cat at home, they can get a can of food to go. And if they don't have a cat at home, they can adopt one of ours! This is a *great idea*.

When we're done, I turn to the chair behind the counter. Granny is asleep! And Bubbles

and Pepper are both snoozing in her lap!

A few more customers walk in. The bell on the door rings and startles Granny awake. Bubbles and Pepper look at me grumpily. "That wasn't *my* fault," I protest.

Granny turns the music down a little so she can hear the customers. The first one in line leans down and stares at the bakery case. Dozer hops off the stereo, onto the top of the bakery case, and swishes her tail.

"How can I help you?" Granny asks.

The customer keeps staring at the bakery case. He looks confused as he taps his fingers on the counter. *Tap tap tap. Tap tap tap.* "Hmm," he says. "Hmm-mm-mmmm."

"Cat got your tongue?" Granny says, and then she laughs so hard at her own joke that her dentures fly out of her mouth. They land on the register. I see Dozer crouch like she's going to pounce on them!

"Don't even think about it, Dozer," I say. She shows me her teeth.

I pick up the dentures and hand them back to Granny. "Sorry about that," I say to the customer. His eyes are wide and he seems even more confused than before. "Can we help you figure out what to get?"

"Well, I don't eat gluten or dairy or sugar," says the customer. "But it does smell fishy in here. Do you have smoked salmon?"

"Actually it's cat food," I say. "It's for sale! You can feed it to the cats in the café. They're pretty hungry."

"Uh, okay . . ." the customer says.

"Also we have an egg frittata that's gluten and dairy and sugar free. And if you buy a can of cat food, you get the frittata for free!"

The customer's head snaps back toward me. "Really? That's a pretty good deal."

He buys a can of cat food and brings it to the cats while Granny goes to heat up his frittata.

I stand behind the register, feeling proud.

"What's this I hear about free food?" another customer asks.

"You get something free from the bakery

case if you buy a can of cat food," I say.

"And if you buy a can of cat food, you get something else for free," Ryan says seriously. He comes to join me behind the counter.

"What's that?" the customer asks.

"The joy of feeding a cat that needs a home," Ryan says.

I give him a fist bump under the counter. Turns out, the suit is making him into a pretty good businessperson!

We sell a *lot* of cat food after that! Soon The Purrfect Cup is full of happy customers and happy cats. And it smells fishier than ever. Almost every table is full! And Granny is pretty good at getting the line to move along fast.

Maybe it's because she keeps dropping her dentures on the counter, which makes some customers want to order their cat pies to go.

I chase after Dozer, who's still more interested in human food than cat food. She runs up to the door just as it swings open again.

"Hey," a boy calls out. "What happened to the music?"

I look up and see the boy and the woman from this morning. They came back! And they brought their whole family. I count nine people.

Uh-oh. Where are they all going to sit?

5

Families and Frenemies

"Hi," says the boy. "I'm Manuel Bautista. This is my mom, my dad, my sisters, my brother, my aunt, my grandpa, and my grandma!"

"I'm Kira Parker," I say. "That's my brother, Ryan, and my granny. My parents are out of town. That's why my granny is here."

"Your grandma doesn't live with you?" Manuel asks. "That's weird."

"Do your grandparents live with you?"

"Of course." He gestures at his family. "But this is not all the Bautistas. Only the ones who live with us."

"You all live together?" I ask. "My aunt doesn't even live in this state! We only get to see her on holidays."

"Who do you hang out with?" Manuel asks. "Don't you get lonely?"

"Not really," I say, looking around the café. "I hang out with my cats! They're my best friends."

Manuel nods. "That makes sense. There are so

many cats here. That's the one thing I'm missing. An animal! We have a lot of humans in our house but no pets."

I smile. "Then you came to the right place."

I crank the music back up and take the Bautistas' orders. Ryan and I bring extra chairs up from the basement and push tables together so Manuel and his family can sit down. I wipe a bunch of sweat off my forehead, which means I need to wash my hands again so I can bring food to the tables. This is a lot of work! I walk back to the kitchen to wash my hands.

"Kira, while you're back there, can you fix me a plate?" Granny asks before ringing up the next customer. "I'm getting hungry for lunch."

I sigh. "Sure, Granny."

When I come back out with clean hands and a plate of food for Granny, there's chaos in the middle of the café! Dozer is all tangled up with an orange tabby cat.

"Are they playing or fighting?" Manuel asks me.

"Looks like they're just *kitten* around," I say, but I'm not so sure. "I think maybe they're becoming friends."

"They look more like frenemies," Manuel says. "Friends and enemies."

I make a face as two more cats join their tangle. I break up the fight, but Dozer doesn't calm down. She hops from table to table.

"That big cat is hilarious!" Manuel's grandpa says. "She's feisty, just like my wife."

"Hey, Kira, can you put back on that song that was playing this morning?" Manuel's mom asks. She gestures to her family. "That's one of our favorite songs to play."

"That's a good idea," I say. "That song helps Dozer calm down. Are you all musicians?"

"A few of us are," she says. "The rest prefer to listen. We play live shows in cafés sometimes. Let me know if you ever need a band!"

She hands me a card with her phone number on it. "Cool, thanks!" I say. "I'll go put that song back on now."

As I walk to the back of the café, another

customer calls out to me from a table across the room.

"Can I get another one of those cute cat pies?"

"I'd love a green tea," says a customer a few feet away.

"Can you close the window?" another man asks. "I'm a little chilly."

"Oh no, please keep it open," says a woman. "It's helping with the fish smell."

I feel frazzled. I imagine myself looking just like Pepper did after she got sprayed by a skunk and had to take three baths in a row.

Then I look at the counter. Granny is sleeping again! The music and the packed café don't stop her from snoring so loud I can hear it from here. I look around for Ryan. He's sitting in the corner with two cats on his lap, working on his cat biographies.

"Hey, partner," I say. "I could use your help!"

He scowls at me and sets his papers aside. "Fine, I'll get the cat pie."

I put on the song from this morning. As soon as I do, Dozer calms down again. She lies on the floor beneath Manuel and closes her eyes. That's one problem solved! Next I let the man and woman switch tables. That way, the one who's cold isn't by the window, and the one who doesn't like the fishy smell can sit right by the breeze. Then I wake Granny up so she can pour the hot water for the green tea.

She blinks slowly. "Hey, Kira," she says. "I think I dozed off for a second."

"Maybe we should call *you* Dozer," I say. "But not because you're a bulldozer. Because you like to doze off a lot."

Granny chuckles. "I'll pour that tea, don't worry. Look who's back to see you!"

I turn around to see Mr. Anderson walking into the café.

"Hey, Kira!" he says. "I wanted to come see how things were going. Ben is watching the shop. Wow, it's busy in here!"

"Yeah," I say, sighing as I plop down into one of

the few empty chairs. "It's been a lot of work. I don't know how you and Ben and Mama and Dad do it! You don't even get a break to go to school during the day."

Mr. Anderson laughs. "That's the first time I've heard someone call school a break," he says. "But you're right. It is a lot of work."

"Yeah, there's so many customers. Plus, there's the new cat, and my new cat food idea, and the music."

"Hmm," Mr. Anderson says, scratching his chin. "You know, when I was first opening Anderson's Artsy Abode, I realized I couldn't do too many things at once. I had all these things I wanted to sell, but it was just too much. So

I started small—we only sold paint at first. Then over time, we added more stuff. Markers and fabric and everything that's in the shop now."

"Really?" I ask. "I can't imagine Anderson's Artsy Abode only having paint!"

"And when your parents first opened this place, before you were born, they only let two cats live here at a time. And there was only one thing on the menu!"

"Was it cat pies?" I ask.

"No, it was something much simpler. The cat pies came later. They are delicious, though . . . think I could get one while I'm here?"

"Of course!" I say, jumping out of my chair.

"And I can get you some cat food to feed the cats. And maybe you'd like to read Ryan's cat biographies—"

Mr. Anderson raises his eyebrows. *Whoops!* I bet he thinks I didn't listen to anything he said. I did, I just forgot.

"How about I start small? Just the cat pie?"

"That'd be great."

But then Ryan walks up behind me and whispers in my ear. "Uhh, Sis, we just ran out of cat pies. I gave that other customer a blueberry muffin instead. But we're going to run out of food soon. I think your cat-food idea worked a little *too well*."

"Oh no," I say. "What are we going to do if we

don't have food to serve the customers? Should we call Mama?"

I feel uncomfortable. I think about what Mr. Anderson said about taking on too much at once. Maybe I have been trying to do too much. I don't want Mama to know I've been using too many *great ideas*, but she should know if the café is going to run out of food.

Ryan nods seriously. "We should also tell her about Dozer."

I use the café phone to dial Mama's number. But it rings and rings before I remember.

"Mrs. Patel told them to turn off their phones! What do we do now? The customers are getting restless. They're all asking about the cat pies."

"We could entertain them," Ryan says.

My brain moves fast. "Yeah, maybe that could work. You should read one of your cat biographies to the customers!"

Ryan smiles wide. He stands up on a chair in the packed café and clears his throat.

"Hello, everyone," he says. "I want to take a

moment to tell you about our newest cat in the café! She has a beautiful, thick coat of white fur, and she is one of the biggest cats we've ever seen. She loves frosting and fighting. She's very clumsy, like my sister, Kira. Her name is Dozer because she's like a bulldozer, as you can see . . . uh-oh."

As Ryan talks, Dozer seems to notice that all eyes in the café are on her. And she *loves* the attention! A little too much. She leaps from table to table. The customers pick up their mugs and plates so she won't knock them over. Then she lands in front of Manuel. She sits down, stares right into his eyes, and—BAM! She uses her paw to knock his glass off the table. It shatters on the floor. Manuel covers his face, and Dozer goes back to fighting with one of the other cats.

I look down at the broken glass, then up again at Manuel's covered face. I like Manuel and his family. I hope they're not so mad they leave The Purrfect Cup.

But before I can say sorry and offer them free tea, the bell at the front of the café rings again. *Oh no.* Not more customers! They won't be happy if we have no food *and* no glasses to serve water in.

I turn around and see Alex and Mrs. Patel in the doorway. Their eyes are wide.

Mrs. Patel looks over at the broken glass, the

fighting cats in the middle of the room, and the almost-empty bakery case.

"Oh dear," she says, pinching her nose. For the first time, I think it's not because of her allergies. The fishy smell isn't great.

I look back to Granny for help.

"What's the matter?" she asks. "Want me to order a pizza?"

"No," I say. "I want to take a cat nap."

6

The Cat Nap

The Purrfect Cup is finally quiet. I lie down on the floor in the middle of the café and sigh. Dozer pounces onto my chest.

"Not now, Dozer," I say. "I'm exhausted."

Dozer prances away. Pepper walks up to me and snuggles in the space between my head and my neck. She makes a pretty perfect pillow.

Ryan hangs a sign in the door that says:

Closed for a Cat Nap.

Some of the customers were pretty confused when we said that we were closing for a few hours. But Mr. Anderson helped us get everyone out, and I told them all to go shop at Anderson's Artsy Abode instead. And the Bautista family promised they'd come back to the café tomorrow, so at least I didn't lose all my customers. We didn't even have to ask Granny for permission to let us close—she started snoozing as soon as I said "cat nap"!

Alex lies next to me on the floor.

"How did that kid from your article run his own restaurant?" I ask. "It's so hard. You know how I never let the cats look at lasers?"

"Yeah," Alex says. "You always say you're on the lookout for lasers so you can protect them. I've never seen any lasers in this town, though."

"Well, you never know when they might show up."

Alex nods seriously. "That's true," she says. "Lasers are sneaky."

"And the reason I need to protect the cats is because it *seems* like they have fun chasing lasers on the wall, but really they're being forced to run in all these random directions!

And they never get to catch the laser at the end. That's what being in charge of the café feels like. Chasing something I can never really catch. I have so many *great ideas* but no time to put them to use!"

"Maybe the kid who owns his own restaurant is a super genius with two brains and six hands and eyes on the back of his head," Alex says thoughtfully. "Or he gets a lot of help from his parents."

"I wish I had an extra set of hands and eyes," I say.

"Well, I have hands and eyes," Alex says. "So does Ryan, and your grandma, and my mom! We could all help!"

"That's true," I say. "But I wanted to show Mama that I could run the café. I want her to be proud of my *great ideas.*"

"Your mom *loves* your great ideas!" Alex says. "I think she's just been busy."

"Yeah, maybe . . ." I say.

Mrs. Patel calls to us from the doorway. "Hey, girls, what's that you're saying about great ideas? Kira, the town council wants us to put on more events where people from our community can get together. You're always thinking of ideas! Maybe you and Alex can cook something up."

"See! Everyone loves your ideas. *Especially* your parents," Alex says. Then she yawns. "I think I'll take a cat nap too. But I'll do it at home. Call me if you come up with any ideas that could help my mom! Or if you need help from us. We've got four eyes and four hands."

"Thanks, Alex," I say. "That'd be great! I'll call you soon."

I turn back to Mrs. Patel to say goodbye. She's shooing Dozer away, but Dozer won't listen. Dozer looks at Mrs. Patel, who looks back, like they're guarding each other in a basketball game. When Mrs. Patel moves one way, Dozer moves the other to try to get around her. She wants to escape! Mrs. Patel shifts the other way again quickly, then sneezes.

"I could use some help over here!" she calls out.

Alex stands up and walks over to Dozer. She picks her up and sets her on a chair inside the café. "Dozer, this is your home now. Don't worry, Kira is going to take care of you and the café. She just needs you to take a cat nap so she can make a plan. She's really good at that."

"Thanks, Alex," I say. "See you soon?"

She nods and leaves. Dozer seemed to listen to her. She hops onto a cozy spot in a cat tree and lies down. She doesn't stop staring at me, though.

"Dozer, glaring at me is not going to help me nap or figure out how to run the café better. You're creeping me out!"

In response, Dozer shows me her teeth. I put

my head back on the floor, but only for one second because the café door opens again.

"Hi," says a woman, poking her head inside. "I heard you were giving away free food with a cat food purchase."

"We're out of food," I say. "Both the cat and human kind. And we're closed."

I point to the sign. The woman reads it. "'Closed for a Cat Nap.' I thought that was a joke." She sighs. "I guess I'll have to go somewhere else?"

"Yes, you will," Ryan says, walking back into the café. The woman raises her eyes when she sees his suit. She must know he means business because she leaves. Ryan locks the door behind her.

He looks at me. "This is impossible! There are too many customers!"

I nod in agreement. "It's im-paw-sible. Maybe we should stay closed the rest of the weekend until Mama and Dad get back."

"Maybe," Ryan says.

"Where'd you go, anyway?" I ask. "When Alex and I were lying on the floor."

"Bathroom," Ryan groans.

"Breakfast cupcakes were a bad idea."

"Yup."

"Want to bring a bunch of pillows downstairs so we can take a cat nap in the middle of the café?"

Ryan smiles. "I thought you'd never ask!"

We wake up an hour later, covered in cats. As we slept, they all crept closer and closer to us, finding spots by our knees and elbows to snuggle in. They make me feel warm and cozy, and for a little while I forget all about the mess we made in the café today. Dozer comes to cuddle by my feet, and I don't even mind that she licks my shoes for, like, ten minutes straight. There's nothing better than napping with a whole bunch of cats!

"What's that smell?" Ryan asks, yawning.

I take a big whiff. I smell cats, and cat food, and coming from the kitchen . . . buttery sweetness wafting over our heads.

I sit up straight. The café may be closed, but *something's* cooking.

7

Baking Basics

I stretch my arms and walk slowly into the kitchen. I still feel a little groggy from the cat nap. But as soon as I see the kitchen, I feel wide-awake!

There are bowls *everywhere*. They're all filled with different ingredients, and they sit on the counters in neat, organized lines. Granny stands in the middle of the kitchen, weighing flour into bowls with a scale. She hums a sweet lullaby as she works.

"Granny, what are you doing?" I ask. "I thought you and Bubbles were resting."

"Kira, you know *mature* people don't need to sleep for long! We like getting our beauty rest here and there, but we don't sleep for hours like you kids."

"I forgot that was true about old people. But you're right, Mama and Dad almost never sleep for long."

Granny shakes her head. "Those two need a little more beauty rest, if you ask me," she says. "I wish they'd take some cat naps!"

She pours tiny bowls of baking soda and salt into the flour bowl, then whisks it all together. Then she carefully folds the dry ingredients into a bowl of wet ingredients.

I sit on one of the kitchen stools. "Granny, I didn't know you were a baker."

She looks at me like she can't believe the words that are coming out of my mouth. "Who do you think taught your father everything he knows? I should have taught him a little more, mind, because he sure makes some dry cat pies."

I laugh. "Granny, why do you keep saying that about Dad's pies? I think they're perfect! Plus, they got us famous on the internet."

She gives me side-eye, then puts on an oven mitt and pulls a pie out of the oven. It's shaped like a regular pie, not a cat, but the top crust is decorated with cat-shaped cutouts. Underneath the cutouts, I can see a thick layer of bubbling blueberry filling.

"Wait for this to cool down, and then you'll see," she says.

I don't want to wait. The blueberry pie looks and smells *so* good. Pepper and Bubbles come into the kitchen and sit on my lap. I don't want to disturb them, which makes it easier to sit still. I watch Granny as she hums and measures and mixes. She's so careful about everything.

"Why do you set all the ingredients out in

separate bowls?" I ask her. "I don't think Dad does that."

"I like to be prepared before I start the real baking," she says. "And then I follow my recipes, one step at a time. That helps me keep things in the kitchen calm and clean."

I've never been very good at keeping *anything* calm and clean. I had a lot of *great ideas* today, but I wasn't prepared for any of them. I brought the cat food out without thinking about how it would stink up the café, I let Dozer run loose with cats she didn't know, and I turned the music up loud without thinking about how early in the morning it was. Maybe that's why everything went wrong. My ideas were great, I just needed a better plan!

Granny slices the pie. She sets a piece in front of me. It's warm and not too sweet and the flaky crust melts in my mouth. I didn't think anything could be better than Dad's pies. But I was wrong.

"Oh," I say.

"Yeah." Granny nods. "*Oh* is right."

"If you're so good, why did Dad bake the pies

for the weekend? We could have had you bake everything!"

"Because perfection isn't the goal. Learning is the goal. And your father's got to keep baking so he can keep learning. I'm proud of his dry pies. They're much better than they were a few years ago!" She chuckles. "Besides, I'm a granny. I like spoiling my grandbabies and supporting my children. Can't do that if I'm always taking over in the kitchen."

Granny leans in close. "But I have a hunch that he knew I'd end up doing some baking. I can't help myself—I love it. Even if we hadn't run out of food, I'd have still been back here eventually."

"Do you think he also knew that we'd have to close the café because one of the cats bulldozed it?"

Granny raises her eyebrows. "No," she says. "I don't think anyone could have predicted that. But you did a good job today, Kira. I mean, you're only one tiny person. Look how much you accomplished on your own! You figured out that Dozer calms down with music, you kept your customers happy, and you sold a *lot* of baked goods with that buy-one-get-one-free idea."

"I'm not tiny!" I protest. "I'm almost as tall as you."

"That's only because I've shrunk. That's what happens when you've been alive as long as

I have. But listen to what I'm saying. If you did all that today on your own, imagine what you could do with a team helping you out."

I take another bite of pie. "Do you really think I can run the café without messing everything up?"

"Of course I do. I think you *and* Ryan can. Just think of the café like a recipe that needs to be followed very carefully."

I nod. "This time we'll be more prepared."

I'm not giving up on my *great ideas*. But I'm going to try again more slowly and take everything one step at a time.

It's time to get some more eyes and ears.

8

The Sound of Mewsic

The café stays partly closed for the rest of the day.

When Granny's baked enough goods, Ryan adds

an extra line to his sign on the door so it says:

Closed for a Cat Nap.

Open for Takeout.

Ryan and I take turns bringing Granny's baked goods out to the customers. A lot of people show up! They stand in front of the window and watch the cats while they eat their treats. When there aren't any customers, Ryan and I sweep up the mess in the café. Once everything is sparkling clean, we start to plan for tomorrow!

I think about what Alex said about the kid who opened a restaurant. She said he probably needed extra hands or extra help from his parents. I bet he does a lot of work himself, but that doesn't mean he has to do *all* the work! And Granny told me that she believed I could run the café if I had a team. I don't need to do everything by myself to impress Mama. It's better to learn a little bit at a time, the way Granny bakes, and to ask for help when I need it.

I tell Granny that I'm going next door to talk to Mr. Anderson. After all, Mama did tell us we could go to him if we needed anything.

I walk into Mr. Anderson's craft shop, Anderson's Artsy Abode. Inside, it smells like paper and fresh flowers. Looking at the neat shelves filled with brightly colored pencils and paints makes me feel calm and cheery.

"Hey, Kira," Mr. Anderson says. "Sorry things got so tough this afternoon. I hope you've been having fun, though."

"One cat was having a little too much fun," I say. "So we closed for a cat nap."

Mr. Anderson smiles. "That seems like a good idea."

"I wanted to talk to you because I think we're going to have some more music tomorrow. Would that be okay?"

"Of course!" Mr. Anderson says. "Is there anything else I can help you with?"

"Actually, there is," I say. "Do you still have that tie-dye kit? Can you show me how to use it?"

"I sure can."

When Mr. Anderson and I are done with the tie-dye part of my plan, I move on to the next step in my recipe plan. I ask Mrs. Patel whether a concert at the café would be a good community-building event. She says yes! Mrs. Patel says that the town council can pay Manuel and his family to play a show at the café if they're available. *And* she's going to help spread the word about the concert. I take out the card Manuel's mom gave me and call to see if they're available for a show tomorrow. They are!

I'm so excited that when it's time for bed, I can hardly sleep. But Granny reminds me that sleep is an important part of all plans and I can't skip any steps, just like in a recipe. I know that's true because one time I was making Dad's brownie recipe and I skipped the line where it said to whisk the eggs. I just dropped them in whole, and the brownies came out with chunks of scrambled egg inside. I don't want anything like that to happen tomorrow, so I curl up with Pepper and close my eyes.

♥ 🐾 ♥

In the morning, I remind myself to take things step by step and to be prepared! I show my tie-dye project to Ryan—T-shirts that say *The Purrfect Cup*! We set them out on the shelves with a little sign showing that they're for sale. Then, we fill the bakery case with Granny's blueberry pies, and this time, we remember to feed the cats before the café opens. But I put a sign up by the counter that says:

Cat food cans for sale.

All proceeds go to the King County Animal Shelter.

Please don't open the cans indoors because they

smell.

After all, why *shouldn't* a cat café sell cat food? I still think that was a *great idea!*

Then Ben and Mr. Anderson come over to help us rearrange the furniture in the café. We push chairs and tables together to save space—and so that people in the community can get to know each other while they listen to the music. We leave a big area open in the corner by the window for the Bautistas and all their instruments.

There's a knock on the door. It's the Bautista family! And they're carrying their instruments.

"Good morning," I say. "I'm so happy you could come play today! We set up a spot for you in this corner by the window."

"Great!" says Manuel's mom.

"How's my favorite feisty cat?" Manuel's grandpa says. He looks around for Dozer. She's high up on a shelf, napping next to Bubbles.

"Actually, she's doing great!" I say. "She's been a lot calmer today. I think she just needed some time to get used to the space. And she really loves music! I bet she can't wait to hear you all play."

Manuel's aunt reaches up to scratch Dozer's ears. "She's a good kitty. She just has a lot of energy, like us! Do you have some tea with honey? I need to warm up my vocals."

"Of course!" I say. I serve the tea in paper to-go cups so there's no chance of any more broken glass.

The Bautistas set up guitars, a cello, and a keyboard. Manuel pulls a violin out of a case and starts to tune it as other people arrive. There isn't an empty seat in the house!

"Thanks for spreading the word, Mrs. Patel," I say when she and Alex come by.

"Of course," she says. "Thank you for this wonderful idea! This is going to be great for the community. And the first of many shows, I hope. Is there anything else we can help with? I say *we*, but I mean Alex. I'm going to drop her off. I have to swing by the store to pick up my allergy medicine."

"Sure!" I say. Alex takes orders for tie-dye T-shirts. Ryan serves thick slices of blueberry pie, and everyone tells Granny how delicious it tastes. I walk around, clearing tables and making sure everything is going according to plan. If this day was a blueberry pie, I think it'd have the most perfect, flaky crust *ever*!

Manuel gives me a thumbs-up when the Bautistas are finished setting up their instruments. I move to the front of the café.

"Thank you all for coming to The Purrfect Cup's first-ever live concert!" I say. "We're excited to have the Band of Bautistas playing for us. This show is put on by our town council. And remember, all the cats you see are available for adoption! Except Pepper and Bubbles, of course. My little brother, Ryan, printed out biographies for all the adoptable cats. They're in a stack near the counter if you'd like to take one."

The customers clap while the Bautistas start to play. They make the music sound even better than the record! When the cats hear the music, they stand up on their back legs and sway along with the rhythm. It's so cute, all the customers take out their phones and start snapping pictures! Dozer hops onto Manuel's

lap and meows as he sings. Then she tries to play his violin. Manuel laughs.

When the Bautistas are finished playing, everyone in the café cheers! A man with a deep voice says, "One more song! That was wonderful."

I recognize that voice! I turn around to see

Dad and Mama standing in the doorway. They're back from vacation! Ryan and I run over to give them hugs.

"How was your weekend?" Dad asks.

"It was *great!*" I say. "Well, we did have to close the café for a while to take a cat nap. And you're going to need to buy some more water glasses."

"'Closed for a Cat Nap,' huh?" Mama says, seeing Ryan's sign on one of the shelves. "You know, that's not a bad idea. Your dad and I were just saying we should take more time off as a family. What do you think?"

"That'd be awesome!" Ryan and I say together.

Dad raises his eyebrows, looking behind me. "Who is that giant cat?"

Manuel walks up to me, holding Dozer.

"That's Dozer," I say. "She arrived yesterday. She has a big personality."

"And I love her," Manuel says. "We want to adopt her and call her 'Mewsic.' Do you have an application?"

"Really?" I say. "I thought you wouldn't like her because she knocked over your glass yesterday. I saw you cover your face."

"I covered my face so you wouldn't see me laughing! I thought that was *hilarious*."

I help Manuel with the application. When we're done, he hugs Dozer and promises he'll be back to bring her home as soon as Mama finishes looking over their adoption papers. Then the Bautistas each give Dozer a kiss on her head. I get a new idea! The Bautistas all play in a band together. Maybe our whole family can work at the café together, including Granny!

She comes out from the kitchen. Dad gives her a hug. "Something smells good in there, Mom," he says. "I knew you'd get up to some baking."

I give Granny a big hug. "I love you, Granny," I say. "I wish we saw you more. Do you want to live with us? Manuel's grandparents live with him. You could stay here and show Dad how to make even better blueberry pies."

Dad's eyebrows shoot up.

Granny hugs me back. "Kira, baby, I love you so much. And like I told you, I'm here on this earth to spoil you. But no, I do not want to live here. Me and Bubbles like our space. Besides, I'm still young and good-looking," she says, dancing a little bit. "I can't waste my youth teaching your father how to cook."

She winks at him. Dad rolls his eyes, then he says, "Love you, Mom. We'll see you soon."

I put a soft blanket inside a cat carrier for Bubbles. She climbs inside and lays down. I think she's ready to go to her new home! Ryan carries the cat carrier while Dad helps Granny walk to her car. Mama looks around the café.

"I see quite a few of your ideas around here, Kira," Mama says. "I thought I told you to hold off on your ideas this weekend."

"I'm sorry," I say. "But I wanted to show you that my ideas could help the café. I was worried that you didn't think I could run a café, so I thought if I did it while you were gone ..."

"Oh, Kira," Mama says. "I'm sorry I haven't made time for listening to your ideas lately. But I have always loved them, and they *always* help the café. You've done some wonderful work here."

"Yeah, and it was a *lot* of work," I say. "I couldn't do it alone. I needed help from Granny and Ryan and our friends. My team."

Mama smiles. "Kira, you're wiser than me! It only took you one busy weekend to learn when to ask for help. Meanwhile, I'm only just now realizing that I should have asked for help a long time ago. Your dad and I have been trying to take on too much on our own. We should ask for help more often. That was a great concert. Maybe you'd like to become our full-time event planner."

Mama winks. I know she's kidding. "You know, I think I'm more of an ideas person and less of a planning person. I'll leave that part to you, for a while at least."

"Oh, really?" Mama laughs. Then she sees the look on my face. "Wait, don't tell me you're coming up with *more* ideas right this second?"

I smile. "I might be."

Read on for a sneak peek at

Kira's next *great idea* in . . .

Two Fur One

"Welcome to The Purrfect Cup, the best and only cat café in town! Can I interest you in a ca-*purr*-cinno?"

The customer standing in front of me looks confused and nervous. Probably because our family's cat, Pepper, is sitting on the counter staring at him. Her tail is perfectly still and her eyes don't blink. Pepper lifts her paw and licks her claws slowly, never taking her eyes off the customer.

"Um, can I just get a cup of water?" he asks.

"Sure, I guess," I say. "But if you change your mind, we also have hot chocolate with marsh-*meow*-lows. Or I could make you some *purr*-itos and avo-*cat*-o toast."

"Kira Parker," Mama says sternly. "What are you going on about?"

Mama joins me behind the register. She pours a cup of water for the customer. "Sorry about that. We're actually all out of our homemade marshmallows. And we've never served burritos or avocado toast," she says.